Mr. Sweetums Wears Pink

Story by
Charlotte Hutchinson

Art by
Brenda Jones

RAGWEED
THE ISLAND PUBLISHER

Story © 1991 by Charlotte Hutchinson
Illustrations © 1991 by Brenda Jones

To Carolyn and Garbo
with thanks for the inspiration

To my family and friends
who care enough to comment and criticize constructively

10 9 8 7 6 5 4 3 2

With thanks to the Canada Council for its kind support

cover & book design:
Brenda Jones,
Lynn Henry
editing: Lynn Henry
printing: Wing King Tong Co. Ltd.
in Hong Kong

Canadian Cataloguing in Publication Data
Hutchinson, Charlotte, 1949-
Mr. Sweetums wears pink
ISBN 0-921556-18-7
I. Jones, Brenda, 1953- II. Title.
PS8565.U82M7 1991   jC813'.54   C91-097529-9
PZ10.3.H87Mr 1991

Ragweed Press
P.O. Box 2023
Charlottetown
Prince Edward Island
C1A 7N7

Mr. Sweetums was not a happy cat. He was a well fed and well loved cat, but he was not a happy cat. He longed for a different life, a better life.

Sometimes he imagined being called Percival and living with very rich people. He thought he would enjoy being pampered.

Then again, the name Spike appealed to him.

He could live in an alley
with lots of other cats.
He'd be the meanest, roughest,
toughest feline on the fence,
under the moon.

Hiss,
claw,
murowww!

He even thought it would be okay
to be named Lucky and belong
to a fun little boy or girl.

Then he could
romp,
tumble
and play.

Anything, yes anything, would be better than being named Mr. Sweetums and belonging to three of the frilliest, frothiest, flounciest, fluffiest, sparkliest, pinkest little girls you could ever imagine.

The three sisters loved Mr. Sweetums, and they loved to play with him. They played teacher and pupil and dressed him up in cute school clothes. He hated that.

They played doctor and patient and dressed him up in adorable pyjamas. He hated that more.

But worst of all, they played mother and baby. They dressed him up in pink baby clothes with lots of lace, frills and ribbon. They tied a bonnet on his head and put booties on his paws. Then they wrapped him up in a fluffy pink blanket, rocked him and sang lullabies.

As if that weren't yucky enough, sometimes they took him outside for a walk in the stroller. He'd burrow down in the blankets and wish, wish as hard as he could, that none of the other cats would see him.

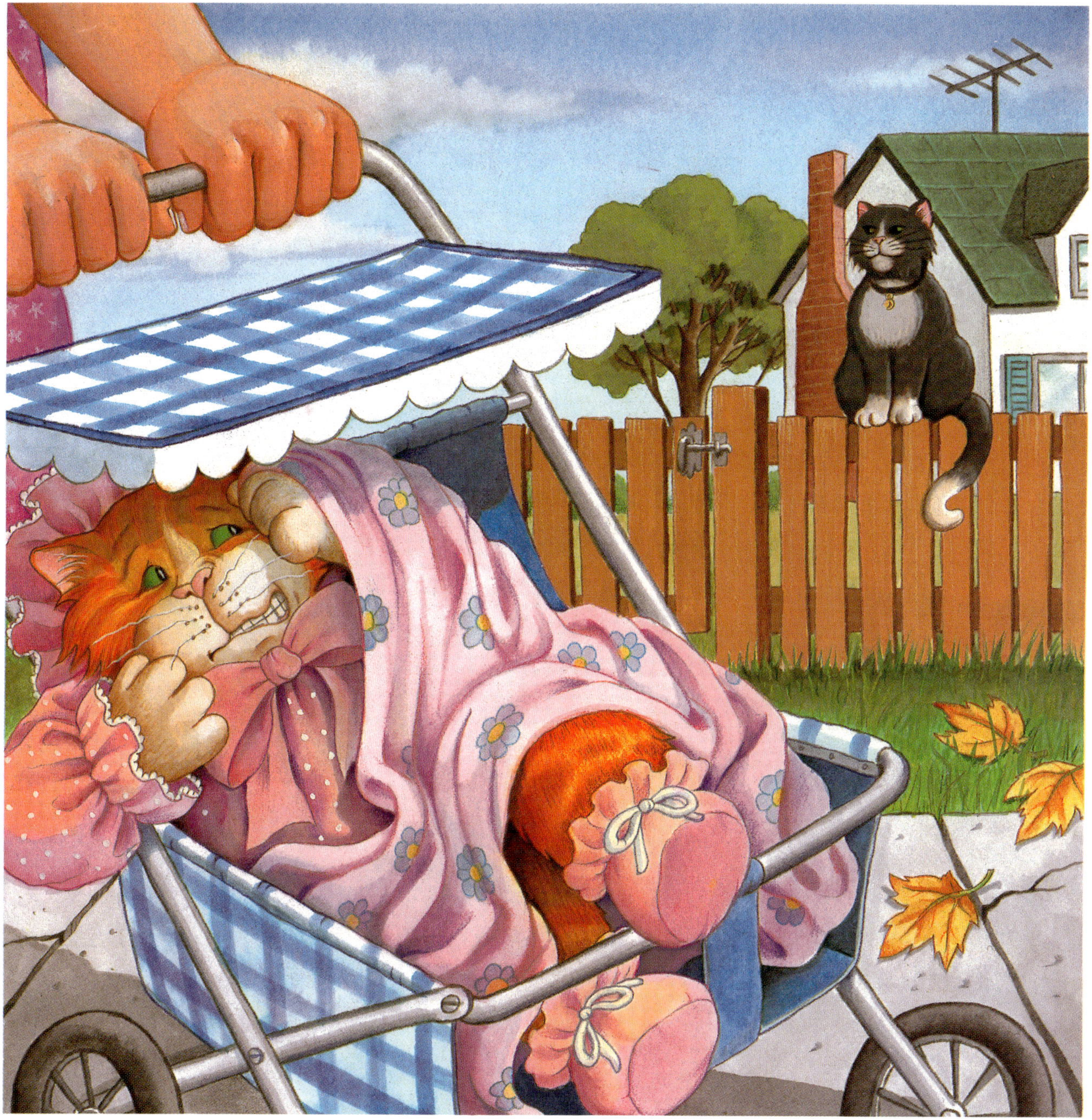

The only time the girls left him alone was when they practised their ballet. They dressed up in their pink, frilly tutus and danced, danced, danced.

Sometimes Mr. Sweetums would watch them in disgust. Other times he'd have a lovely nap in the sun and dream of life as a Percival, a Spike or even a Lucky.

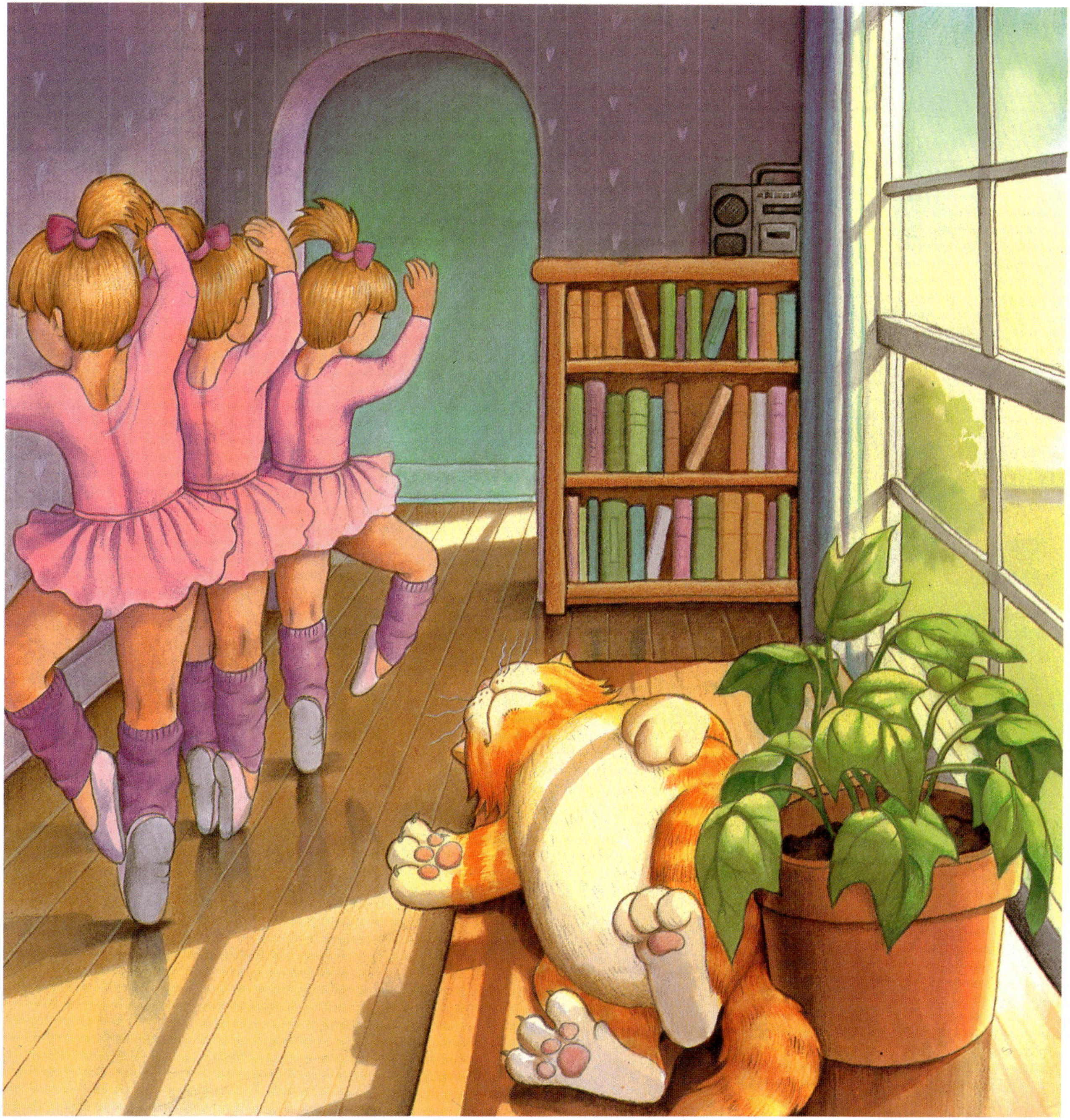

One afternoon Mr. Sweetums heard the girls whispering and giggling. He caught words like, "party," "surprise," "costume," "tonight" and "Mr. Sweetums."

Mr. Sweetums started to worry. The more the three sisters whispered and giggled, the more he worried.

Then the girls rushed into their bedroom and slammed the door. Mr. Sweetums could hear more whispering and giggling. At last the door flew open.

At first he thought three giant cotton candies had escaped from the circus, but then he realized it was the three sisters bouncing around in the frilliest, frothiest, flounciest, fluffiest, sparkliest, pinkest ballet costumes in the entire universe. Mr. Sweetums felt sick.

Then he saw IT.

His heart went clunk in his chest. He gulped.

IT was a frilly, frothy, flouncy, fluffy, sparkley, pink ballet dress, and it was just his size. He let out a terrible yowl and ran for his dignity, ran for his tomcathood. He ran down the stairs, up the walls, across the ceilings, down the walls, over the furniture, around the rooms and back up the stairs.

Three pink clouds chased after him. Finally they trapped him in a corner.

Mr. Sweetums lay helpless as they dressed him in the tiny pink gown. He shuddered as they tied two tiny pink satin ballet slippers to his hind paws. He gasped as they buckled a jewelled velvet collar around his neck and attached a pink leather leash.

Poor Mr. Sweetums.

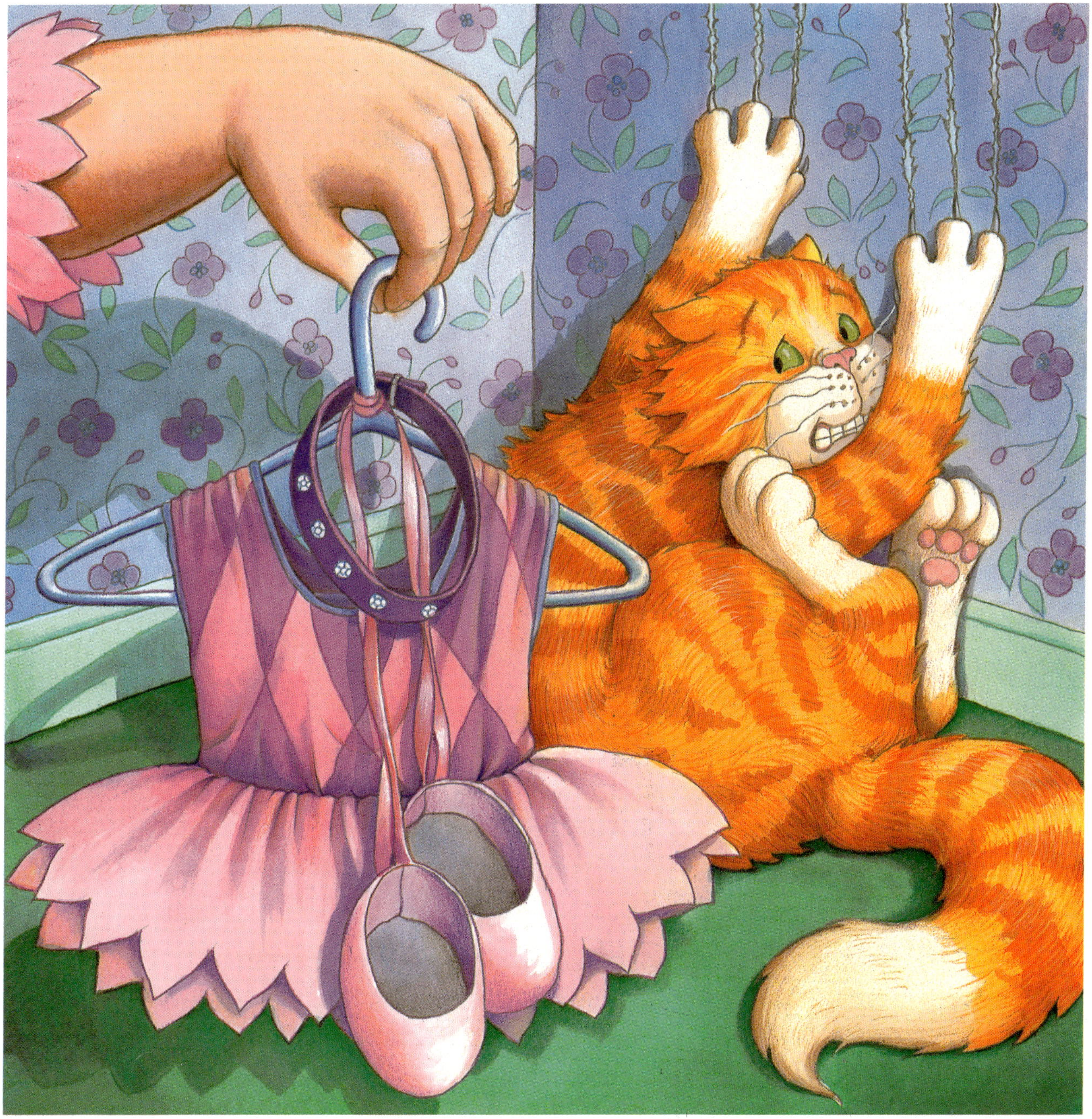

Soon the pink fluff balls set off for the party pulling Mr. Sweetums on the leash behind them. He put his head down and tried to be invisible. He hoped that none of the other cats would see him.

At the party Mr. Sweetums hid under a chair and tried to look as small as possible, but the girls kept pulling him out to show him off to the other guests. "Oh, isn't he just adorable," they said, "He's bound to win a ribbon."

Little Tammy Tottle arrived dressed as a witch, carrying her black tomcat, Tommy. Mr. Sweetums was horrified to see one of the neighbourhood cats at the party, but at the same time felt smug that he was wearing a costume. "Some idea," he sniffed, "bringing a black cat disguised as a black cat. That will never win a ribbon."

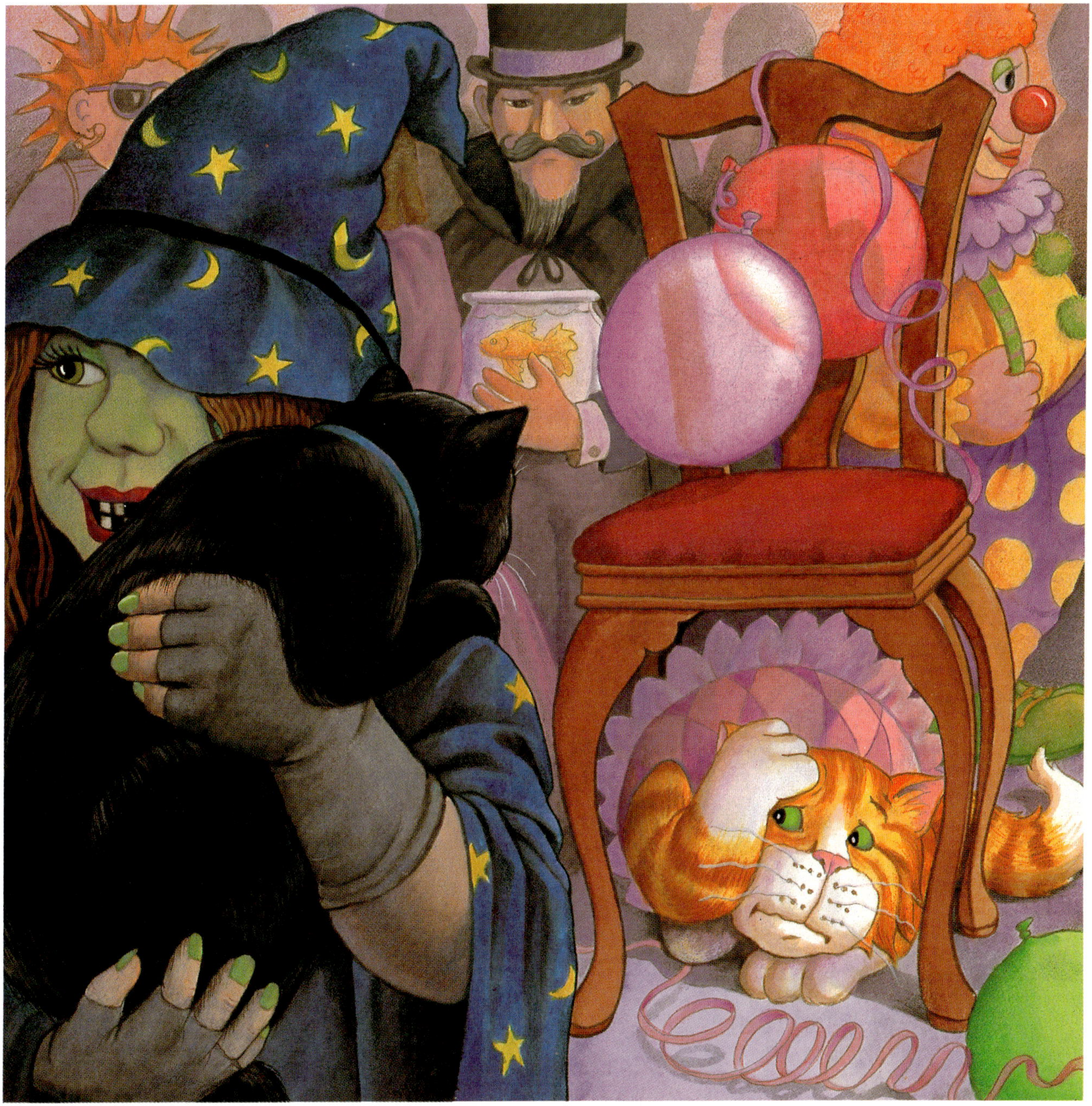

When refreshments were served, Mr. Sweetums was well looked after. He had all the tuna fish sandwiches he could eat, and ice-cream served in a bowl. And what do you think happened? In spite of himself Mr. Sweetums found he was liking all the attention. He started to hope he might win a ribbon.

Soon the contests were held. To the delight of Mr. Sweetums, the magician who swallowed the fish came first in the talent contest. The three sisters entered the frilliest, frothiest, flounciest, fluffiest, sparkliest, pinkest costume contest. "Who else even has a chance?" thought Mr. Sweetums. So he wasn't surprised when a shiny red ribbon was pinned on each of the girls. But he was quite surprised when a ribbon was pinned on him too.

Then came the category for the most adorable pet. Mr. Sweetums did his best to please the judges. He fluffed out his costume and pointed his ballet slippers. Then he tilted his head to one side and gave a deep "murrowww!"

A big cheer arose and a second shiny red ribbon was pinned on his collar.

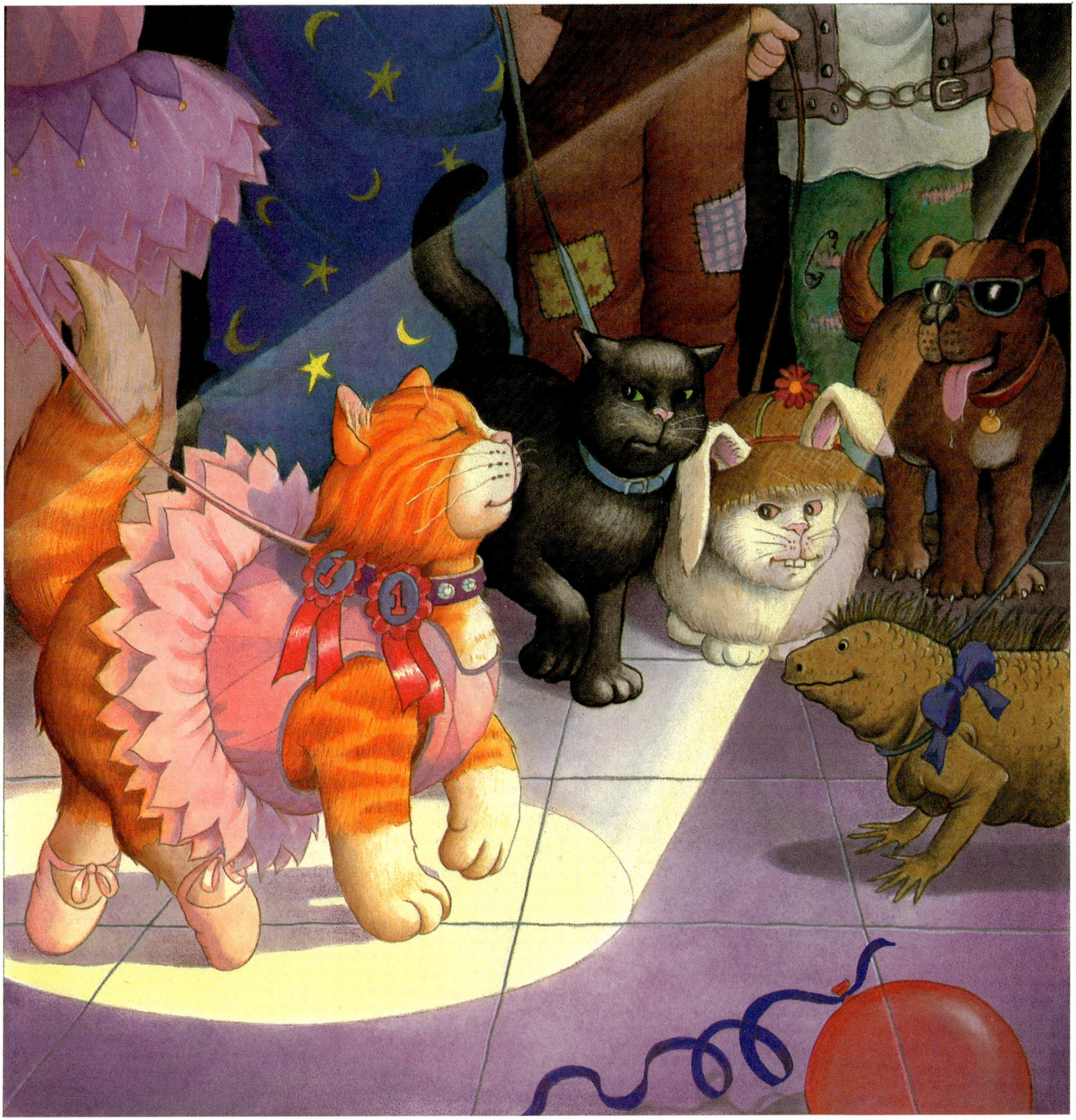

Finally the evening was over and the girls carried home an excited but tired Mr. Sweetums. On the way, they nuzzled him and told him he was the most special cat in the whole world. He snuggled in close and purred, not caring who saw or heard him.

When they reached home the girls kissed him good-night and headed off to bed.

Earlier in the evening Mr. Sweetums had planned to tear off his costume the minute he could, but for some reason he didn't. His tummy felt good, and he looked down and admired his ribbons again. He remembered the nice snuggle on the way home. He lay down.

Then the music started in his head. It began very softly, but soon got louder and louder. Before long one of his tiny pink satin ballet slippers started to twitch. Then the second slipper moved. Soon his whole body began to sway. An uncontrollable urge brought him to his feet.

Mr. Sweetums stood in the middle of the living room, threw out his paws and started to dance. And, oh, how he danced.

He whirled on his toes. He spun from one end of the room to the other. He leapt onto the coffee table. He danced around the rims of the lamp shades and over the backs of chairs.

He tried to remember all the things he'd seen the girls practice. Then he tried new steps of his own. Not once did he think about the other cats in the neighbourhood. He danced and danced and danced as the music played on.

Finally, exhausted, he collapsed on the floor. He fell asleep with a smile on his face as the music faded away.

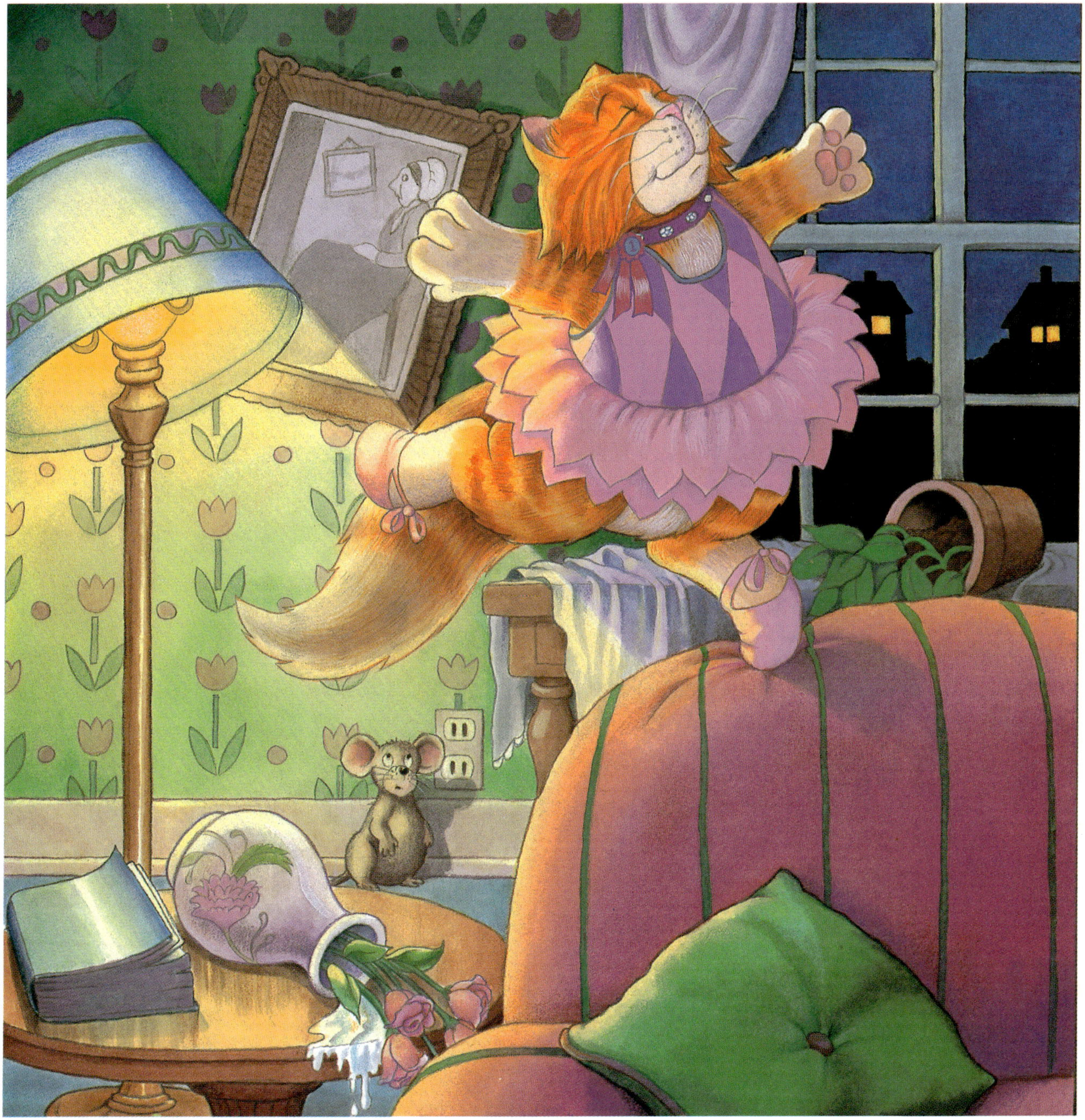

Now, since that night, things have changed quite a bit for Mr. Sweetums. He doesn't get too upset when the sisters dress him up and play with him—except for that baby outfit, of course.

He hardly ever wonders what the other cats think. Seldom does he dream about life as a Percival, a Spike or a Lucky.

You see, Mr. Sweetums lives to dance.

When the three girls practice their ballet, Mr. Sweetums stays awake and watches. He pretends not to, but he really does watch—very carefully.

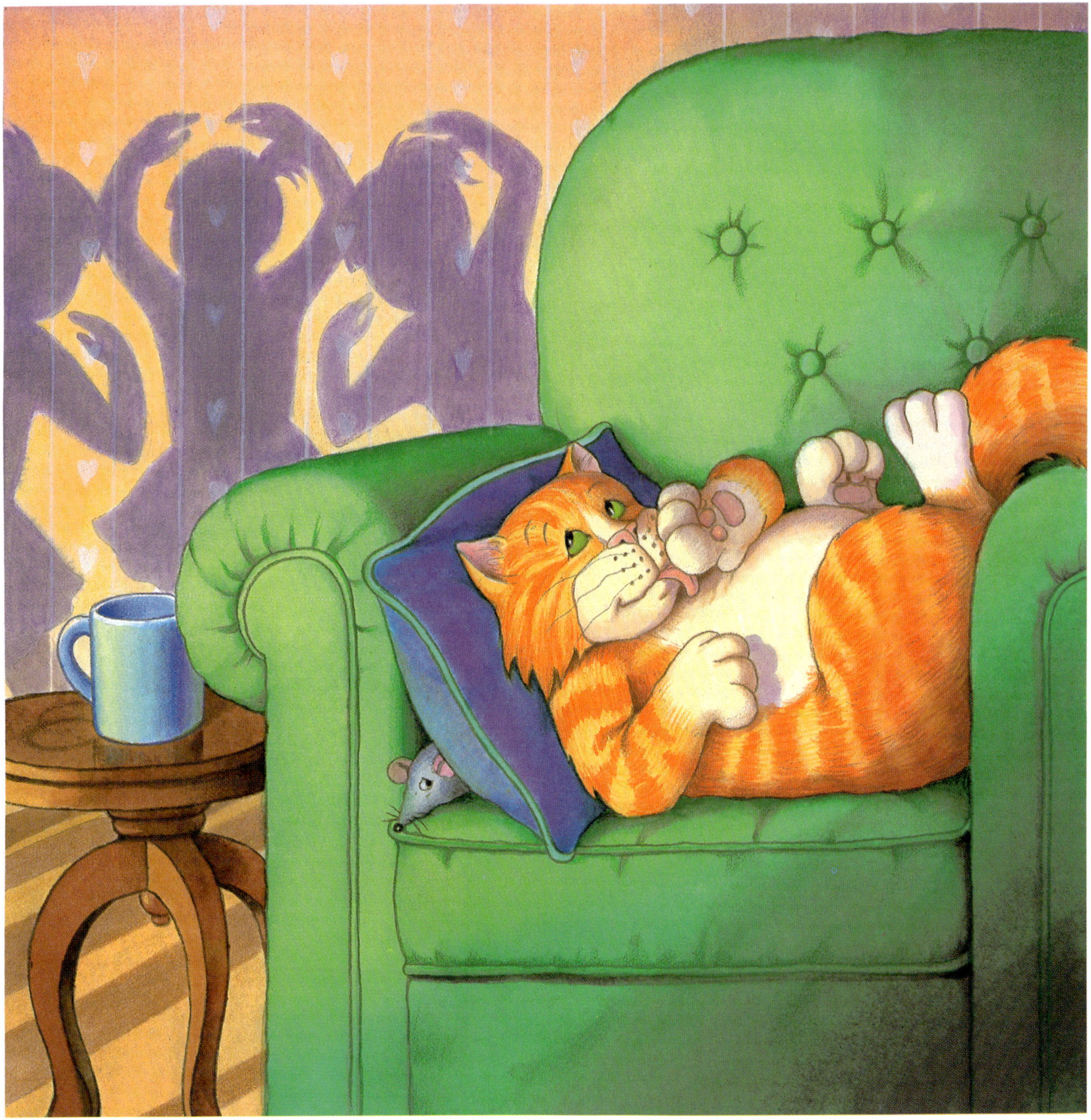

Then late at night, when he's all alone, and the music starts up in his head, Mr. Sweetums dances.

And he dances and he dances until he's too tired to dance even one
        more
                step.